Ruth
the Red Riding Hood Fairy

by Daisy Meadows

ORCHARD

www.rainbowmagic.co.uk

The Fairyland Palace

Fairyland Library

The Three Bears' Cottage

Island

Thumbelina's Cottage

Storybook World

Rapunzel's Tower

Red Riding Hood's Grandmother's House

Red Riding Hood Woods

Jack Frost's Spell

The fairies want stories to stay just the same.
But I've planned a funny and mischievous game.
I'll change all their tales without further ado,
By adding some tricks and a goblin or two!

The four magic stories will soon be improved
When everything soppy and sweet is removed.
Their daft happy endings are ruined and lost,
For no one's as clever as handsome Jack Frost!

Contents

Fairy Tale in the Firelight

"There's something so magical about a campfire," said Kirsty Tate, warming her hands as the flames flickered.

"I love staring into the flames," said her best friend, Rachel Walker. "If you gaze at them for long enough, you can start to see pictures in there."

The girls leaned against each other, feeling happy, sleepy and relaxed. They had spent a wonderful weekend at the Wetherbury Storytelling Festival, but now it was Sunday evening and the fun was nearly at an end. Together with the other children from the festival, they were sitting on logs in a circle around a campfire. Alana Yarn, one of their favourite authors, had helped to organise the weekend, and she was sitting on a log too. The girls had had a wonderful time getting to know her.

"So," said Alana, looking around the circle at them all. "Have you enjoyed the Storytelling Festival? What was the best bit?"

Everyone nodded and started to call out their favourite moments.

"The only bad thing about the whole weekend is that it has to end," said Rachel.

Alana smiled.

"We still have one more storytelling session before you have to go home," she said.

There was a large wicker basket in front of her, and she began to rummage through it.

Rachel turned and smiled at Kirsty.

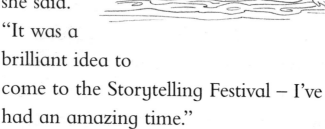

"Thank you for inviting me to stay this weekend," she said. "It was a brilliant idea to come to the Storytelling Festival – I've had an amazing time."

"You're welcome," said Kirsty. "I'm really glad you came. I enjoy everything ten times more when you're here. It's been an extra-special weekend."

Rachel nodded.

"Especially because we've had such

a wonderful time with the Storybook Fairies," she whispered.

Rachel and Kirsty had shared lots of secret adventures with fairies, and meeting the Storybook Fairies had been enchanting. Elle the Thumbelina Fairy had whisked them away to the Fairyland Library, where they met Mariana the Goldilocks Fairy, Rosalie the Rapunzel Fairy and Ruth the Red Riding Hood Fairy. They were all very upset because Jack Frost and his goblins had stolen their magical objects, but Kirsty and Rachel had already helped get three of them back.

"I just hope that we can get Ruth's magical basket back soon," said Kirsty. "Until then, Jack Frost still has control of her story."

The fairies' objects gave the holder power over each story. Elle, Mariana, Rosalie and Ruth always used their objects to make sure their fairy tales unfolded correctly. But Jack Frost and the goblins wanted the stories to be all about them. They had been using the magical objects to go *into* the stories and change them.

"We've got three of the objects back so far," said Rachel, thinking about their adventures during the festival. "There was Elle's thumb ring, Mariana's spoon and Rosalie's hairbrush. If only we had already found Ruth's missing basket! Without it, I'm worried that Alana's final storytelling event will be ruined."

Just then, Alana Yarn cried, "Aha!" and pulled a red hooded cloak from her basket. She threw it around her shoulders with a flourish, and put up the hood. Her eyes twinkled in the firelight as she gazed around at the children. For a moment, no one spoke. They could hear the crackle of the burning twigs on the campfire. As the sun set behind the hills, the moon and stars began to shine.

"To close the festival, we are going to do something very special," Alana said. "Everyone is going to tell a story together. We will pass this cloak around the circle, and whoever

has it will tell part of the story. Does anyone have any questions?"

"What else is in the basket?" called out a girl with blonde, curly hair.

Alana smiled. "There is a surprise inside my basket, but that's for later. Right now, we have a story to tell!"

Kirsty and Rachel looked at each

other, knowing that they were thinking the same thing: *Please don't let Jack Frost and his goblins ruin the story!*

Scrambled Story

"Let's begin," said Alana in an excited voice, taking out a red book and turning to the first page. "This beautiful cloak I'm wearing is a clue to which story we're going to tell. I will start you off, and let's see where the story takes us! Once upon a time…"

She passed the cloak and the book to the girl next to her, who put on the cloak and carried on reading from the book, "...there was a little girl called Red Riding Hood."

The boy next to her took the cloak and book and continued, "One day, her mother asked Red Riding Hood to take some cakes to her grandmother."

As the red cloak and the book were passed around the campfire circle, the story of Red Riding Hood unfolded and Rachel and Kirsty began to relax. Everything was happening exactly as it should. Perhaps Ruth had already managed to find her magical basket! They listened as Red Riding Hood set off through the wood to her grandmother's house with a big basket of goodies. Then the red cloak was passed to Rachel.

Feeling excited, Rachel slipped the heavy red cloak around her shoulders. It felt warm and she closed her eyes for a moment, thinking about all the things that she had learned about storytelling that weekend. Then she opened her eyes and started to read out the next part of the story.

"Red Riding Hood was halfway through the wood when she saw three figures on the path ahead. They were goblins!"

Rachel clapped her hand over her mouth, and Kirsty gasped in horror.

"Rachel, she meets a *wolf* in the woods, not goblins!" Kirsty whispered.

"I know!" Rachel groaned. "But the book says 'goblins'! And somehow I couldn't stop myself from reading it out!"

She quickly passed the cloak to Kirsty, who pulled it on and took the book, hoping that she could read the story without saying the word 'goblin'.

"Red Riding Hood knew that she shouldn't speak to strangers," Kirsty began, "but the goblins said – oh!"

Now it was Kirsty's turn to clap her hand over her mouth. She also hadn't been able to stop herself from saying 'goblins' instead of 'wolf'!

The girls gazed around at the other children, but no one seemed to have noticed that anything strange had happened. Kirsty didn't dare to try again. She took off the cloak and passed it and the book to the children on the next log.

As a little boy put the cloak around his shoulders, Rachel nudged Kirsty.

"Look at Alana's basket!" she whispered.

The basket was glowing as if there was a fire inside it. The girls watched and saw a tiny fairy flutter out of the basket and shoot into the air.

"It's Ruth the Red Riding Hood Fairy!" Kirsty exclaimed.

Ruth was wearing a white skater dress with red stars around the hem, and a silky red cloak was swirling around

24

her shoulders. She had beautiful glasses with delicate black frames, magnifying her sparkling eyes.

Her brown hair gleamed in the firelight as she zoomed down to the girls and hid behind the log where they were sitting.

"Hello, Ruth," Rachel whispered out of the corner of her mouth. "It's good you're here – something very strange is happening to the *Red Riding Hood* story."

"I know," Ruth whispered back. "I need

your help – and quickly! Will you come
into the story with me now?"

The girls looked around at the other
children. Everyone was gazing at a boy
who was reading out the next part of the
story.

"The goblins snatched Red Riding
Hood's basket and blew a big raspberry
at her," the boy was saying.

"Oh dear," said Kirsty in a low voice.
"We really need to find those goblins.
Luckily, no one's looking our way. Come
on – let's go!"

Moving slowly so they wouldn't attract
attention, Rachel and Kirsty slipped off
the log and ducked out of sight. Ruth
gave them a relieved smile.

"I already feel better just knowing
you're going to help me," she said. "Elle,

Mariana and Rosalie all said that they couldn't have got their magical objects back without you."

"We're just happy to be able to help," said Rachel. "We don't want the last event of the Storytelling Festival to be spoilt. We want to save stories for everyone!"

Ruth took out a little red book. The words *Red Riding Hood* were written in silver letters on the front, and they sparkled in the light from the campfire. Ruth held up her wand and spoke.

"The storybook world is in danger today.

We must find the goblins and send them away.

*Take me and my friends to the path
through the wood,*
    *And help us to rescue dear Red Riding
Hood."*

The campfire, the other children and
the twinkling stars disappeared as if
someone had blown them away. Instead,
Rachel and Kirsty found themselves
standing on a narrow, winding path,
surrounded by crowded fir trees on both
sides. They were inside the storybook
world once more.

Tracking
the Goblins

Ruth fluttered between Rachel and
Kirsty as they gazed around. In the
storybook world, the girls were still
human sized. Bright sunlight filtered
through the leaves, and bluebells and
poppies grew in colourful patches among
the trees.

"How beautiful," said Kirsty.

"Listen!" Rachel exclaimed, putting
a hand on her friend's arm. "I can hear
someone coming."

The girls darted out of sight behind
a tree, and Ruth perched on Kirsty's
shoulder.

Seconds
later, a
little girl
came
skipping
around
a bend in
the path.

She was swinging a wicker basket as she
skipped, and her red cloak swirled around
her shoulders. She was singing a song to
herself.

"Red Riding Hood!" Rachel whispered in a thrilled voice.

"She's such a happy girl," said Ruth with a smile.

Suddenly there was a cacophony of screeches, squeals and whoops, and three goblins leapt out of the wood and capered around Red Riding Hood. She gasped and turned from left to right, trying to get away from them. But one of the goblins grabbed at her cloak.

"No, that's mine!" she cried.

But the goblin just laughed at her and pulled the cloak from her shoulders. Her basket was knocked to the ground, and cakes, buns, biscuits and fruit scattered all around. The goblins ran off into the wood, shrieking in delight.

"Hey, stop!" cried Red Riding Hood. "Bring back my cloak! Thieves!"

She started to chase them, but she tripped over a tree root and fell onto the leafy ground.

Rachel and Kirsty darted out from behind the tree and helped Red Riding Hood to her feet.

Her knees were dirty and her pinafore dress was torn.

"Are you all right?" Kirsty asked.

"Yes, I'm fine," said Red Riding Hood. "They just gave me a surprise. My mother warned me that there were wolves in the wood. She didn't say anything about strange green creatures like that."

"They're so mean," said Rachel. "Don't worry – we'll help you pick up your things."

Kirsty and Red Riding Hood gathered armfuls of the fruit and cakes, and Ruth picked up the checked cloth that had covered all the food. Rachel picked up the basket, which had rolled to one side of the path, and looked at it carefully. Her heart gave a sudden hopeful thump of excitement.

"Ruth, could this be your magical basket?" she asked.

Ruth shook her head.

"Mine glitters with magic," she said. "Besides, we know that Jack Frost and his goblins have it."

The girls packed the food back into the basket, and then Ruth tucked the checked cloth over everything.

"Thank you," said Red Riding Hood. "You're very kind. But oh dear, I'm so sad to have lost my cloak. My grandmother made it for me, and I always wear it."

"The goblins have stolen something belonging to Ruth, too," said Kirsty. "We have to get it back! If we can catch them, we will get your cloak back too."

"Thank you!" said Red Riding Hood. "But I must hurry – my grandmother will be waiting for me."

Red Riding Hood waved and went on her way. As she disappeared along the winding path, Rachel heard a distant, high-pitched giggle.

"Goblins!" she exclaimed at once. "I'd know that sound anywhere. If we're quick, we can still catch up with them."

"They might lead us to your magical basket, Ruth," Kirsty added.

"Good thinking," said Ruth. "And wings are quicker than feet!"

She waved her wand, and a shower of silvery sparkles erupted from the tip. Showered in fairy dust, Rachel and Kirsty twirled around as they shrank to fairy size. Their delicate wings unfurled

and fluttered, shaking the last sparkles
of fairy dust onto the path through the
woods.

They rose into the air and listened.
Somewhere ahead of them, among the
crowds of trees, the goblins were still
giggling.

"Come on, we mustn't lose them!" cried
Ruth.

They flew over the treetops, guided by the giggles. Soon they spotted the three goblins below. One of them was wearing the red cloak and pretending to be Red Riding Hood, skipping along and singing in a silly, squeaky voice. The others were shrieking with laughter and jumping around, pulling faces.

"Those naughty goblins!" Kirsty exclaimed. "I wonder where they're going."

"Let's get closer," said Rachel.

They weaved among the trees, staying

behind the goblins and listening as they giggled and teased each other. Then they reached a clearing, where a tall oak tree was growing among the firs. A blue hammock swung from the branches, and the goblins stopped and stared at it. The fairies stopped too, their wings fluttering fast as they hovered.

"Why have they gone so quiet?" Ruth asked in a whisper.

The hammock moved, and the goblins took a step back. Then a pair of familiar, angry eyes peeped over the hammock's edge.

"About time!" snarled Jack Frost, sitting up.

"Oh my goodness!" Kirsty cried. "Look what he's got on his lap."

It was Ruth's glittering magical basket!

41

Twisted
Hammock

"We have to get it back," Rachel said in a determined voice. "Come on!"

The three fairies swooped down towards the basket, hoping that they could reach it before they were seen. But the goblin in the cloak glanced up and spotted them.

"Ooh!" he squeaked, jumping up and down and pointing. "Ooh! Ooooh!"

Jack Frost looked up and rolled his eyes.

"Stop saying 'Ooh!', you nincompoop!" he snapped. "They're fairies, not fireworks!"

He clutched the basket to his chest and pointed a long, bony finger at the fairies.

"You lot clear off!" he shouted. "Swat them away, goblins! Get them!"

Kirsty dived under the hammock and the goblin in the cloak lunged after her.

Kirsty darted out of his way, and he hurled himself against the hammock by mistake.

"EEEK!" yelled Jack Frost as the hammock spun over and over, wrapping him up inside it.

"WAHHHH!" wailed the goblin as Red Riding Hood's cloak was tangled into the hammock.

Seconds later, when the hammock stopped spinning, Jack Frost and the goblin were knotted together, their legs and arms sticking out at all sorts of peculiar angles.

"We should grab the basket while he can't use his hands to stop us!" said Ruth.

"The basket is buried somewhere inside that hammock," said Kirsty. "We'll have to wait."

She led Rachel and Ruth up to a tree branch above.

"How are we ever going to get my magical basket back?" Ruth asked with a groan.

Rachel and Kirsty couldn't answer, because Jack Frost was shrieking too loudly, his voice getting higher and higher with each word.

"How dare you tie me up? Who did this? When I get out of here you lot are going to be in so much trouble!"

The goblin in the red cloak was also yelling, but his voice was too muffled to be understood. The other two goblins hid behind the oak's trunk, their knees knocking together.

"Those poor goblins," said Rachel. "It's not their fault that he got all tangled up.

47

I know they're naughty, but they don't deserve to be shouted at like that. Jack Frost needs a good scare of his own."

"That gives me an idea," said Kirsty. "I know who would scare Jack Frost – the wolf!"

"You're right," said Ruth, looking thoughtful. "And the best person to help lure the wolf to where we want him is Red Riding Hood herself."

"Yes!" said Rachel, clapping her hands together. "If we can get the wolf to come to the oak tree and scare Jack Frost, we might be able to grab the magical basket."

"Come on, there's no time to lose!" Kirsty exclaimed. "We have to catch up with Red Riding Hood!"

The three fairies zoomed into the sky

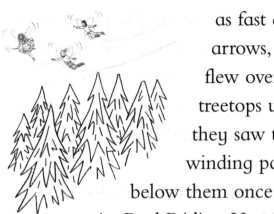

as fast as arrows, and flew over the treetops until they saw the winding path below them once again. Red Riding Hood was hurrying along, but she wasn't skipping now. Rachel, Kirsty and Ruth swooped down and hovered in front of her.

"Oh, hello again!" said Red Riding Hood, frowning a little. "Weren't you human beings a few minutes ago?"

"It's magic," Ruth explained.

"Oh, I see," said Red Riding Hood. "That explains it."

In the storybook world, no one was surprised by magic.

"We've come to ask for your help," said Kirsty. "We want to get the wolf to go to the big oak tree in the middle of the wood. We think he might be able to help us get Ruth's basket and your cloak back from the goblins."

"Will you help us?" asked Ruth. "Please?"

"Of course," said Red Riding Hood at once. "I'll do anything I can to get my cloak back and stop those naughty goblins!"

Frightened Frost

Red Riding Hood and the fairies quickly worked out a plan. Then Rachel, Kirsty and Ruth fluttered up to hide in the treetops.

"Tra la la," sang Red Riding Hood in a loud voice. "I can't wait to see my grandmother! I'm sure she'll love this big basket of goodies I'm taking to her."

The leaves on the other side of the path rustled, and then a large grey wolf stepped out. He bared his teeth and licked them with a long, pink tongue.

"He looks very scary!" said Rachel with a shudder. "What big teeth he has!"

"Where does your grandmother live, little girl?" asked the wolf in a gruff voice.

Red Riding Hood pointed the way through the wood towards the big oak tree.

"Granny lives that way," she said.

The wolf didn't wait to listen to

anything else. With one bound he was charging into the wood, speeding towards the clearing where the fairies had left Jack Frost.

"Quickly – don't lose sight of him!" Rachel cried.

The three fairies flew above him, and Red Riding Hood ran along behind him as fast as she could. The wolf was very fast.

"He'll soon be at the oak tree," said Ruth. "Let's fly ahead!"

They zoomed towards the clearing and saw that Jack Frost and the goblin with the cloak had managed to get untangled, and the Ice Lord was once again relaxing in his hammock.

"Look, he's still got the magical basket!" said Kirsty.

Jack Frost was twirling the glittering basket on the tip of his forefinger, chuckling. Beneath the swinging hammock, the three goblins were busy cheating at Snap.

"I showed them!" Jack Frost crowed. "I showed those silly fairies! They just flew away because they were so scared of me. Ha!"

HOWWWWL! The wolf leapt into the

clearing. Jack Frost let out a high-pitched
squeal and sprang out of his hammock.
The magical basket fell down and rolled
across the ground.

"The basket!" screeched the goblin with
the cloak.

"Never mind that," shouted Jack Frost.
"RUN!"

The goblins darted after him, and in
their panic the cloak dropped on the
ground. Ruth swooped
down to seize her
basket, and
it shrank to
fairy size as
soon as she
touched it.

"Let's get
the cloak!"
said Rachel.

She and Kirsty
fluttered down and picked up the cloak
between them. The wolf howled again,
just as Red Riding Hood arrived in the
clearing, out of breath.

"Here's your cloak," said Kirsty, flying
over to Red Riding Hood.

She and Rachel carefully draped the cloak around the girl's shoulders. Then Red Riding Hood turned to the wolf.

"I'm sorry, she said. "I got muddled up about the direction to my grandmother's house. It's just down that path."

She pointed down a narrow path through the wood, which the fairies had not noticed before. Through the leaves, they could just see the chimney of a little cottage.

The wolf dashed off along the path, and Red Riding followed, skipping slowly and swinging her basket.

"The story is back to normal," said Ruth. "Now everything will start to happen just as it should."

"I hope Red Riding Hood will be all right," said Kirsty. "That wolf really is rather scary."

"Don't worry," said Rachel, smiling at her. "Remember the story? Red Riding

Hood and her grandmother manage to trick the wolf and escape. And we know that will happen, because the magical basket is back with its rightful owner."

"Come on," Ruth said, fluttering over to join Rachel and Kirsty. "We have somewhere wonderful to go!"

Back in the Library

Ruth waved her wand, and the storybook wood around them vanished. They were once again standing in the beautiful Fairyland Library. Rachel and Kirsty gazed around in wonder and delight at the high shelves filled with books and the arched glass ceiling. Standing in front of them were Elle the Thumbelina

Fairy, Mariana the Goldilocks Fairy and
Rosalie the Rapunzel Fairy. Ruth rushed
over to them, and they all hugged her.

She placed her magical basket carefully
into the wooden box where it belonged,
and closed the golden clasp. Then all
four of the Storybook Fairies turned to
Rachel and Kirsty.

"You two have been wonderful," said
Elle.

"All our magical objects are safe again, and we have you to thank," added Mariana.

"We will never forget what you have done for us," said Rosalie.

Ruth stepped forward and gave each girl a kiss on the cheek. She was about to speak, but before she could say a word there was a thunderclap and a bright, icy blue flash. The fairies were dazzled and had to shade their eyes. When they looked, they saw Jack Frost standing in the middle of the library. His frown was worse than ever.

"You've spoiled *everything*!" he yelled. "You interfering busybodies! All I wanted was to be the star of my very own story. I made those stories a million times better and you've ruined them!"

"You can still be the star of a story," said Rachel.

"Not without the Storybook Fairies' magical objects I can't," he snarled. "Give them to me!"

"You *can* be the star," Rachel insisted. "You just have to make up the story yourself. Don't ruin stories that already exist. Make up something new!"

"Everyone loves the fairy tales that the Storybook Fairies protect," Kirsty added. "We can't allow you to change them. But I bet you could make up a brilliant story about your own adventures."

She saw a notepad and a pencil lying on one of the library tables. Smiling, she picked them up and handed them to Jack Frost. He hesitated, and then took them as a grin spread over his face.

"My own adventures," he muttered. "It'll be an epic tale. I'll be a brave hero, surrounded by green fools. Yes, I can see it now! *The Adventures of Jack Frost!*"

He sat down and began to write his own storybook world. With a smile, Ruth turned back to Rachel and Kirsty.

"To thank you for everything you've done for us, we have something very special to give each of you," she said.

She handed each girl a small card. On one side, the cards glimmered with the changing colours of the rainbow. On the other, in golden letters, were the words:

Member of the Fairyland Library

"You will always be welcome here," Ruth said to them. "You may borrow one book at a time, and although you will be able to read it, no one else in the human world will be able to see it."

"Thank you!" said Rachel and Kirsty together, feeling awed.

Ruth raised her wand once more.

"Now it is time for us to say goodbye," she said. "But I hope we will soon see you again – on your next library visit!"

She swished her wand, and the bright library vanished away. It was replaced by twinkling stars and flickering flames. They were back at the Storybook Festival.

Rachel and Kirsty listened in delight as the other children finished telling the story of *Red Riding Hood*. This time, Red Riding Hood met a wolf in the wood, and there was no mention of goblins anywhere. The girls exchanged smiles of relief.

"Who wants to toast marshmallows?" called Alana. "I brought some in my basket."

Soon, the children and Alana were enjoying the sweet, sticky warmth of toasted marshmallows.

"Now," Alana said, licking her lips. "Would anyone like to try out what they have learned at the festival? I would love to hear any stories that you have imagined."

Rachel's hand shot into the air.

"Kirsty and I have a story to tell," she said.

"What's it about?" a little boy asked.
Rachel gave a mysterious smile.

"Magic," she said.

Together, the best friends told a tale
of brave fairies and cheeky goblins. The
other children gasped and laughed as
they listened to the story. When Kirsty
said the words "and they all lived happily
ever after," everyone cheered and clapped.

"That was a fabulous story," said Alana.
"I'm really impressed by your amazing
imaginations!"

Rachel and
Kirsty exchanged
a secret smile.
They knew
that they hadn't
imagined the
story!

"I wonder when we'll have more magical adventures," said Rachel.

"Very soon," Kirsty said, feeling certain. "And I can't wait for the next one to begin!"

Meet the Stroybook Fairies

Can Rachel and Kirsty help get their new fairy friends' magical objects back from Jack Frost, before all their favourite stories are ruined?

www.rainbowmagicbooks.co.uk

Now it's time for Kirsty and
Rachel to help...

Melissa the Sports Fairy

Read on for a sneak peek...

"What are you thinking about?" Rachel
Walker asked her best friend Kirsty Tate.

Kirsty was leaning over the railings
of the boat that was taking them to
Rainspell Island. She was gazing down
at the blue-green waves and her hair was
blowing in the breeze.

"I was thinking about the day we met
on this boat," said Kirsty, turning to look
at Rachel. "It was one of the best days
ever. I found a wonderful best friend –
and I met real fairies too."

Rachel smiled back at her. Together,
they had met many fairies since then,

and had many magical adventures. Now
they were returning to the island for the
exciting Rainspell Games.

"I'm so glad that our parents agreed
to bring us here for the Games," said
Rachel. "We'll even be staying in
Mermaid Cottage and Dolphin Cottage,
just like when we met the Rainbow
Fairies. It's perfect."

It was the start of the summer holidays,
and the girls were looking forward to
spending lots of time together. They could
hardly wait to explore the island's green
fields and sandy beaches again.

"I hope we see some fairies too," Kirsty
added. "It always feels as if there's magic
in the air when we're here."

When the ferry docked, Rachel and
Kirsty were the first passengers to step
onto the island. They gazed across to the

other side of the harbour, where their cottages stood on a golden beach.

"We'll get taxis to take us to the cottages," said Mr Walker. "We seem to have brought more bags with us this time!"

While their parents went to find the taxis, Rachel and Kirsty drew in deep breaths of the fresh sea air and listened to the sound of the waves splashing against the harbour wall.

Read **Melissa the Sports Fairy** to find out what adventures are in store for Kirsty and Rachel!

Competition!

The Storybook Fairies have created a special
competition just for you!

Collect all four books in the Storybook Fairies series
and answer the special questions in the back of each one.

Once you have all the answers, take the first letter from
each one and arrange them to spell a secret word!
When you have the answer, go online and enter!

Who is Kirsty and Rachel's favourite author?

_ _ _ _ _

_ _ _ _

We will put all the correct entries into a draw and select
a winner to receive a special Rainbow Magic Goody Bag
featuring lots of treats for you and your fairy friends.
You'll also feature in a new Rainbow Magic story!

Enter online now at www.rainbowmagicbooks.co.uk

No purchase required. Only one entry per child.
One prize draw will take place on 31/06/2016 and two winners will be chosen.
Alternatively UK readers can send the answer on a postcard to: Rainbow Magic,
The Storybook Fairies Competition, Orchard Books, Carmelite House,
50 Victoria Embankment, London, EC4Y 0DZ.
Australian readers can write to: Rainbow Magic, The Storybook Fairies Competition,
Hachette Children's Books, Level 17/207 Kent St, Sydney, NSW 2000.
E-mail: childrens.books@hachette.com.au.
New Zealand readers should write to: Rainbow Magic,
The Storybook Fairies Competition, PO Box 3255, Shortland St, Auckland 1140

Join in the magic online by signing up
to the Rainbow Magic fan club!

Meet the fairies, play games and
get sneak peeks at the latest books!

There's fairy fun for everyone at

www.rainbowmagicbooks.co.uk

You'll find great activities, competitions, stories and
fairy profiles, and also a special newsletter.

Find a fairy with
your name!